Juicy Central™

Diva

Ayshia Monroe

SADDLEBACK
EDUCATIONAL PUBLISHING

Bein' Good

Blind Trust

Diva

Doin' It

The Fake Date

Fitting In

Holding Back

Keepin' Her Man

Stalked

Tempted

SADDLEBACK
EDUCATIONAL PUBLISHING
www.sdlback.com

ISBN-13: 978-1-61651-671-0
ISBN-10: 1-61651-671-2
eBook: 978-1-61247-643-8

Printed in Guangzhou, China
0812/CA21201147

16 15 14 13 12   1 2 3 4 5

Tia Ramirez was the only girl heading into senior year at South Central High School who did two hundred sit-ups every day at four o'clock in the morning.

"Nishell? Can you count them for me?" Tia snapped on the harsh over-head light. Her bedroom was as spare as a prison cell. She had a bed, desk, chair, and a poster of Mexico City on the far wall. That was it.

"Tia. Come on. It's summer vacation. And it's four in the morning!" her friend Nishell Saunders protested sleepily. She'd slept over at Tia's place. "Whatchu doing? Gettin' in shape for *Ultimate Fighter*?"

Tia stretched out on a rubber workout mat. She wore just panties and a white bra. Her lush dark hair was back in a ponytail. She was barely five foot two and had a cute figure that no one would guess at, since she usually hid it under conservative clothes. Recently, she'd started wearing glasses for nearsightedness but didn't need them for her morning workout.

"This is what I do when I get up." She got a mischievous look in her eyes. "Unless you want to do them with me?"

"No!"

"I didn't think so. Now, are you going to count, or am I going to have to hurt you?" Tia asked with a wink.

"You crazy, girlfriend," Nishell told her, rubbing some sleep from her eyes. "But I'll help you. Show me what you got."

Tia started crunching. Nishell started counting.

"One. Two, three, four—dang, girl, slow down, you trying to set a world record? Eight, nine, ten ..."

With each crunch, the noise in Tia's head quieted; life got simple as her muscles and her body took over. She called this her workout zone, and she loved it. Her workout zone took her mind off the stresses of her life, and especially the coming year, when she'd be a senior at gritty South Central High.

Nishell would be a senior too. The two girls had met at yearbook club, which everyone called YC. At first, it seemed like they had nothing in common. Nishell had a white mom, no dad at home, and used to live in a homeless shelter. Tia and her family were new Americans, having moved here fourteen months ago from Nuevo Laredo, Mexico.

Her parents had begged, borrowed, and scraped enough money together to open a little bakery. They gave new meaning to the words "working hard."

Tia had their work ethic. She was one of the two best students at South Central High School, even though English was her second language. During the summer, she toiled at the Northeast Towers day-care as a counselor, plus helped her parents at the bakery, plus was doing all her summer reading for senior year and starting to think about colleges.

"I don't know any kid who does what I do," Tia thought as she crunched. "Since I'm new in America, I have to work twice as hard to succeed. This is a country of so much opportunity. I can't take that opportunity if I am lazy."

"Fifty-five, fifty-six," Nishell counted in wonder. "Day-um, girl, you got abs of steel! An' everyone at school think you just a brainiac diva."

Tia laughed. "I'm just warming up."

"If I did this many crunches, I'd have abs like yours," Nishell observed.

"Yup."

Nishell giggled. "It ain't worth it."

Tia smiled. Nishell was so beautiful; blessed with curves that she would never have. Guys on the street loved her awesome booty. She was a great photographer, funny, and loyal. Nishell would never turn on her unfairly, the way some of the other girls in YC had turned on her.

The Butler twins, for example. Sherise and Kiki. *I still can't believe they ganged up on me and—*

"One hundred ninety-nine, two hundred!" Nishell declared, as Tia ripped through the end of her crunches.

"All right! Time to run." Tia put thoughts of the Butler twins aside and popped to her feet.

"Tia, you are barely breathing hard," Nishell observed.

Tia was already pulling on shorts, a T-shirt, and running shoes. "Like I said, just warming up. Next is three miles. You coming?"

Nishell stared at her. "You kidding?"

"Nope." Again, Tia got a sly look. "How about I cut it to two and a half. Just for you?"

Nishell hit herself in the forehead and laughed. "At this hour it's enough I remember to breathe. I'll see you when you get back."

Tia glanced at the small alarm clock by her bed. "I do seven-minute miles. It's four fourteen now. See you at four thirty-six."

She stretched one calf and then the other. She loved her morning run. The streets were still dark and quiet except for those folks who rose early—the firemen and the cops, the garbage guys, maids, and hotel workers. People who did their jobs, played by the rules, and earned an honest living.

"Last chance. Sure you don't want to come with?"

"Very sure," Nishell declared.

"The coffee's hot; my parents are in the kitchen," Tia told her. She was already heading out the bedroom door. "See you in twenty-one minutes and thirty seconds!"

Twenty-one minutes later, sweating only a little, Tia let herself back into the half of a duplex that the family shared with some distant cousins. She made her way through the living room to the small kitchen. Downstairs were those two rooms; upstairs were bedrooms for her, her little brother, Tomás—who was still asleep—and her parents.

Most norteamericanos *would call this apartment a dump, but it's a lot nicer than what we had in Mexico.*

She found her parents, Carlota and Manuel, with Nishell at the breakfast table. Her folks were dressed in white shirts and white pants for the bakery. Her mom's dark hair was in a bun. Her father's beard was neatly trimmed. Both were full of energy. Not like Nishell, who wore a T-shirt, jeans, and held her coffee cup to her lips like caffeine was the only thing that stood between her and an early death.

"Good run, Tia?" Carlota asked.

Nishell perked up. "You guys speak English at home?"

"Tia says we need to learn English, no matter how hard it is," Carlota said gravely. "Tia works hard at everything."

Manuel looked at Carlota. "My beautiful wife, it is too early for an argument. But our daughter needs to learn that a person should work to live, and not live to work."

Tia smiled as she sipped her coffee. She adored how her father called her mother "beautiful wife" though they'd been married twenty years.

I want a love like that. Someday.

It wasn't that Tia had no interest in guys. She'd hung out during junior year with Ty Kessler. When Ty went to South Carolina for the summer, they'd decided to just be friends. That was fine with Tia. She knew that guys could be a distraction from family, school, and the future. Those were the really important things.

Nishell put down her coffee and turned to Carlota. "What I want to know is how Tia keeps track of everything she does."

"She didn't show you the list?"

"What list?" Nishell asked.

"Mom!" Tia flushed. This was really embarrassing.

Carlota stepped across the kitchen floor and opened the broom closet door. On the inside of the door was a hand-made, hour-by-hour, day-by-day chart. It listed where Tia would be, what she'd be doing, and what she'd be studying. It covered the whole summer.

"It's the only way we can keep track of her," Carlota admitted.

"If I'm going to win the Big Boss Scholarship for being the best student at South Central High School," Tia explained to Nishell, "I gotta be serious about my time."

Manuel shook his head sadly. "That chart is too much. A teen girl needs to have some fun."

"I don't agree, Dad," Tia declared. Her voice was respectful but firm. "You and Mom gave me a gift by coming to this country. I want to give you a gift too. I want to go to a good college, and then to medical or law school so you two can retire."

"You really care about your family, huh?" Nishell asked.

"Nothing is more important than my family," Tia declared. She stood, knowing that she only had a few minutes to go shower. "They gave me a chance at a new life. I'm going to use it to make them proud."

CHAPTER

2

An hour later, Tia and Nishell were in the front area of the Ramirez family bakery. Called Pasteles Bonitas— "beautiful cakes" in Spanish—it was located on an out-of-the-way side street with cheap rents. Tia did a little bit of everything at Pasteles Bonitas. She baked, she cleaned, she served, and she even helped with marketing. For example, it had been her idea to do a Groupon deal-of-the-day that had brought in a lot of new customers.

The bakery—Tia still thought of it as a *panadéria,* the Spanish word for bakery—looked like a lot of places back in Nuevo Laredo. It had a plate glass window, bright yellow paint, and one of the walls was covered by a huge Mexican flag. The lights were fluorescent; the whole place smelled slightly of bleach.

There were so many improvements that Tia wanted to make to the place. Offer teas and fresh juices, in addition to the coffee they already served. An actual lunch menu. Softer lighting. Wood paneling on the walls instead of paint. Discount cards for repeat customers.

And a smaller flag. I love Mexico, I do. But we are not at a soccer game!

Her folks were baking in the rear kitchen. Tia was getting the front area ready for the first customers, who'd arrive when the doors opened at six a.m.

"Tomás is the lucky one," Tia thought, as she applied glass cleaner on a paper towel to the pastry display case. "He gets to sleep in. Cousin Luis will come by for him at seven."

Once the case was clean, Tia tightened her blue bakery apron and gave Nishell a guided tour of the delicious goods that it held.

"These are *pan dulce*." Tia pointed. "They're amazing. To the right are *cuernos*, *orejas*, and *novias* pastries. All fantastic. *Novia* means sweetheart. Jackson should buy those for you. You're his sweetheart, after all."

"Yeah, I guess." Nishell yawned again.

Tia could see how tired her friend was. There were other breads and pastries to show off, but they could wait. "How about you go in the back and find the couch? Sleep back there. I have, plenty of times."

"Come on. The Bionic Latina does not need sleep," Nishell joked. She had her ever-present camera with her and took a few shots of Tia behind the counter. "Okay. Just a few more pics, then shut-eye."

Nishell took some close-ups of Tia with a *pan de muerto*. It meant "bread of death" but tasted incredible, with a sweet, orange-y flavor. Tia, afraid of the calories, allowed herself one thin slice every few days.

I bet Kiki Butler isn't watching her weight like I am.

Kiki. Grrrrr.

Kiki Butler was also in YC. They used to be friends, but then Tia and Kiki found out they were rivals for a big scholarship. If they finished senior year with the same GPA, they would have to share it.

Kiki asked if we could study together and share the scholarship money. When I said no way—that I intended to be the only winner—it made her mad. Very mad.

A couple of weeks later, Kiki and her twin sister, Sherise, had taken revenge on Tia. Tia had been the yearbook manager. She'd worked harder than anyone, including Sherise, the yearbook president, to make the yearbook great. She'd lost fair and square in an election to Sherise, but she wanted to run for president again in the fall. But in a surprise move at a summer YC meeting, Sherise had fired Tia as manager, right in front of everyone, and installed Kiki in her place.

It was so unfair. I know they did it to hurt me.

I don't let people who hurt me get away with it. Then they'll just do it more.

Tia sighed and wiped down the counter by the cash register. Nishell clicked another couple of photographs, and then yawned one more time.

"Go to sleep," Tia ordered.

"You sure it's okay?"

Tia pointed to the back. "I'll wake you in time for work."

Nishell, who was also a day-care counselor, nodded gratefully. "Thanks, Tia. I'm impressed. This bakery, your workout, your fam, everything."

Tia smiled. "Thanks. How do they say it here in America? 'You do what you have to do.' Right?"

"Right. And what I have to do is sleep," Nishell quipped. "See you in a couple of hours."

Tia grinned as Nishell headed into the back. Nishell kept it real, not like backstabbing Kiki or Sherise.

At six, Tia unlocked the door. Two cops came in for *elotes*, a sugar-coated bread that looked like ears of corn. A landscape crew heading for the suburbs loaded up on coffee and *milhojas*—layered puff pastries with a creamy center. Then a woman from the Tenth Street homeless shelter—the same one Nishell used to live in—stopped by to pick up a huge free box of day-old pastries. This daily donation to the shelter had been Tia's idea too.

"No need to make a big deal out of it, either," Tia thought, as she retrieved the box from the back. "People don't want to feel like beggars. When our neighbors gave us food in Mexico, they just left it on the doorstep at midnight."

After the shelter lady was gone, a new customer stepped into the shop. To Tia's surprise, it was Kiki's boyfriend, Sean King. He wore the blue coveralls of an auto mechanic. Tia remembered that Sean was working at a repair shop for the summer. He was six foot one and skinny, with warm eyes, dark skin, and a broad nose and smile. Tia had always thought he was cute.

"Good morning, Sean!" she called out. Just because she didn't like Kiki didn't mean she should be cold to Sean.

"Wassup, Tia," he said, approaching the counter. "I didn't know this was your family's bakery. Can you hook me up with some coffee and stuff for the guys at the shop?"

"My pleasure," she told him, meeting his warm dark eyes. "I'll give you a great discount too."

Sean nodded. "They say you got good stuff here. But I got no idea what to get; I don't speak Spanish." He met her eyes. "To tell the truth, it's a little weird buyin' from you. 'Cause of ... well, you know."

Tia smiled again, trying to make Sean comfortable. "Hey. How do you say it in English? 'Business is business.' Don't worry about Kiki for three minutes, and I'll hook you up with the best pastries ever."

"Sounds great."

"You fix cars, right?"

"Right," Sean acknowledged.

"How many guys at the shop this morning?" Tia asked. She nabbed a set of pastry tongs and a big brown bag.

"Six."

"Then I'll give you eighteen and charge you for six. Keep the extra money or give it back. Your choice," Tia told him.

"That's really nice of you," he murmured, his eyebrows shooting up.

"I'm a nice girl," Tia told him with a quick smile. "Point to anything that looks good, okay?" She moved down the display counter, filling the bag with churros, tasty apple turnovers, walnut cakes, and the double peanut cookies that were her mom's specialty. Then she poured six cups of coffee and filled a tote with cream containers and sugars.

"How much?" he asked.

Tia made a quick business decision. "Know what? It's on the house. Just come back."

"Are you kidding?" Sean's eyes shone happily. "We'll be here every day!"

"That's what I like to hear," she told him, pleased that Sean was happy with her. That could be helpful. If not right away, then at next year's YC election.

She got an idea that might get him to like her even more. Her parents had an old clunker of a car. It was overdue for some routine work.

"Hey, Sean? Where's your garage?" she asked suddenly. "My folks' van needs an oil change. Can you do that?"

"I'd love to," Sean said with enthusiasm. He handed her his cell. "Put in your digits; I'll text you the address."

"Great," Tia told him. "When's a good time to come in?"

"We're slammed today and closed Sunday. How about Monday morning?"

Tia nodded. "Monday's perfect. I'll see you tomorrow night, right? At the planning party for the street fair."

The next night, the Butler twins had organized a YC barbecue to plan for the annual Twenty-Third Street Fair. The fair was a huge event, attracting a ton of people from all over the state. There were hundreds of booths, and big musicians performed. Tia hadn't gone last year, since she and her family had just arrived in America. This year would be her first one.

Sean nodded. "Word. It's gonna be the bomb. Tone Def's gonna perform, you know."

"I'm excited," Tia told him.

Sean nodded with pleasure. "You okay, Tia. Everyone says you a pain in the you-know-where, but you okay."

"Thanks. See you tomorrow."

"And Monday morning," Sean added.

"And Monday morning," Tia agreed. Sean took the pastries and coffee. Tia opened the door for him and watched him walk away from the shop.

Well, well, well, I wonder what Kiki would think about what just happened.

That her rival might be unhappy made Tia very happy.

CHAPTER 3

N ice out here, huh?" Nishell came up to Tia, who stood by the chain-link fence that surrounded the rooftop patio at the Northeast Towers apartment buildings.

The Butler twins lived there with their mom and stepdad. The Towers had been built in the 1960s. Made of red brick, it cried out for a power-washing, or at least a pounding thunderstorm. Inside wasn't much better than out. The elevator had been stuck, so Tia had to walk up fifteen stories to the roof.

For most people, Sunday was a day off. For Tia, it had been mostly the usual. Up before dawn, work out, open the bakery, change and shower, and study. Today, she added a long bus ride across town to this fair planning meeting. From here she'd go straight to an evening church service, where she'd join up with her parents. They always attended the late service so they could staff the bakery in the morning.

And when I get home, I've still got summer reading to do.

The barbecue was a potluck. The Butler twins' mom and stepfather had cooked up pork ribs, chicken, and burgers, while the YC members had brought sides and desserts. Nishell's boyfriend, Jackson, made cole slaw. Nishell came with cold cucumber soup. Tia brought pastries that had disappeared almost before she put them down.

———

The whole YC was there. For a change, neither Sherise nor Marnyke Cooper—the queen flirts of YC—were showing maximum skin. Sherise wore a pink flowered sundress, while Marnyke had come in capri pants and an orange tank top. As for Kiki, she wore her usual basketball clothes and kicks, with her hair in long braids.

Nishell had on brown cargo pants and a black leotard top. Tia was the most formally dressed. She wore a dark jeans skirt and a button-down white blouse that she'd been careful not to drip on while she was eating. She had to look nice for Mass.

The YC men were eating and laughing on the opposite side of the rooftop. Jackson ran the show, telling stories and cracking jokes. With him was Sean, Sherise's boyfriend, Carlos Howard, and a dude named Lattrell

Chance, who seemed to have no life other than to shoot baskets and be Jackson's wingman.

The only person missing was Ms. Okoro, whom everyone called Ms. O. She was the YC advisor and an English teacher at the high school. She was away on vacation in San Francisco.

"You think Marnyke's boyfriend's gonna show?" Tia asked Nishell. Marnyke's boyfriend was a mega-rich white rock-and-roller from the suburbs named Gabe.

Nishell scoffed. "Are you kidding? Come here? To the projects?"

"I guess not. But I imagine Marnyke can be very, um ... convincing."

"With her clothes off, for sure," Nishell cracked. "You gonna be okay tonight?"

"Why wouldn't I be?" Tia tried to deflect the question. Mostly, she didn't want to think about it. The more she thought about it, the madder she'd get. Sherise and Kiki had been hateful to her and had gotten away with it. It was so unfair.

" 'Cause Sherise done dumped your ass as yearbook manager, that's why," Nishell pointed out.

"I'll be fine." Tia looked over at Sean, who caught her eye and gave a little wave. She waved back at him.

Nice. Very nice.

"Hold on. You wavin' at Kiki's man?" Nishell asked.

Tia shook her head with a grin. "No. He's waving at me."

A moment later, Sherise started the formal meeting. Everyone moved benches and chairs into a circle so that Sherise could work the center like a talk-show host.

"Okay," Sherise said once the kids had quieted. "Next Saturday is the street fair.

For those of you who don't know what it is—Tia, I'm talking to you, and I'm talking slow so you'll understand—it's the biggest street fair in the state. Maybe the whole country."

Tia's face burned. She understood English perfectly, now. Sherise was just pushing her buttons. It made her want to push back more than ever.

"There'll be, like, twenty thousand visitors," Sherise went on, turning in a slow circle as she talked. "Community groups can set up booths to raise money. Yearbook club has been invited. I'm gonna ask Kiki, the new and improved yearbook club manager, to talk about some ideas for our booth. Kiki?"

Everyone applauded, except Tia. She fumed at the "new and improved yearbook club manager" crack.

Kiki stood, thanked Sherise, and started explaining some idea for a game where people would pay a buck to guess at the number of M&Ms in a huge jar. The winner would take home five hundred dollars.

Tia thought it was the lamest concept ever. When Kiki was done detailing her ideas, Tia raised her hand.

"Yes, Tia?" Kiki's voice was cold, like she'd rather call on a dead cockroach.

"Those are interesting ideas, Kiki, but we can do better. If it's a hot day—and let's face it, it's July, it's going to be a hot day—those M&Ms are going to melt into goo. Then everyone will guess, 'One!', and we'll have five thousand winners. I know you're doing good tutoring all those kids, but I don't think even you have money for that."

The group laughed. Kiki looked unhappy. Tia plunged on.

"As for the beanbag toss I heard you mention—isn't that for little kids?"

"You have a better idea?" Kiki asked. Venom dripped from her voice. "Tee-yuh?"

Tia tried not to take the bait. "Actually, I do."

Tia stood and stepped into the center of the circle, as if she were still yearbook manager instead of Kiki. "We do the work and set up not just one booth, but four booths. First booth, we bring in a basketball hoop and let people challenge our men to three on three. Jackson, Carlos, and Sean are all great. So's Lattrell. Then we set up a booth where Sherise and Marnyke can do makeovers for the women. They're amazing at that. We do a photo booth where Nishell can take portraits. And finally, we make a soak-the-sap pool, where people can pay to dunk a dork."

Tia's eyes lit up as she thought of a way to make a joke at Kiki's expense. "Hey! That'd be perfect for you, Kiki!"

Again, her classmates roared with laughter.

Lattrell howled. "Kiki just got owned!"

There was a round of clapping that made Tia feel great.

Kiki gritted her teeth, but she managed a reply. "Fine. The city closes Twenty-Third Street on Wednesday," she declared. "I'll send everyone a schedule. That's it, I guess. Thanks for coming."

The meeting broke up. Tia was flying. Four booths was a lot. But they'd have four booths if she had to put them all up herself. She wanted the other YC kids to see how useful she could be. Tonight, they'd seen it firsthand.

"Nice one," Jackson came over to say. "You smart, Tia."

"She the smartest tonight, that's for sure," Marnyke added.

"I hope you're planning to run for president next year," Lattrell told her.

"Of yearbook club?" Tia asked.

"I was thinking of the United States!" Jackson quipped. He got a loud burst of laughter for that. Then those kids moved away and Sean approached. He seemed a little wary. Then he motioned for Tia to follow him over to the block-house that housed the rooftop air conditioning unit.

Ah. Tia realized that on the far side of that structure, they wouldn't be seen.

"Nervous about Kiki?" she asked when they were between the blockhouse and the fence.

"A little," Sean acknowledged. He wore black shorts and an open gray paisley shirt. Tia saw he had some powerful pecs for a thin guy.

"Let's not get you in trouble." Tia couldn't help it. It just felt good to be alone with Kiki's boyfriend. "Unless you wanna be."

Sean smiled. "You still bringing in your car tomorrow?"

"Bright and early," Tia promised.

"Good," Sean told her. "I'll be ready for you."

"I think you're the kind of guy who's always ready," Tia said.

"You got great ideas," Sean told her. "You proved that tonight. Tomorrow, we'll see how your engine feels."

Tia laughed. "Sean King, are you flirting with me?"

Sean grinned. "I can't wait to get my hands under that hood. See you in the morning."

CHAPTER

4

The next morning, Tia did her workout and breakfast routine, then helped her parents open the bakery. At eight o'clock, Carlota said she'd handle the front counter while Tia brought the van to the shop.

Tia wanted Sean to change the oil, yes. But as she'd headed over, she realized that she wanted more. Especially after last night, when Sherise and Kiki had been so mean to her.

If they're not going to be fair with me, they can't expect me to be fair with them.

She knew that one way to get back at Kiki would be to make a friend of Sean. It wasn't that she wanted to steal him away from Kiki. Not that she could steal him away, even if she wanted to. It would be enough if they were friendly. Then maybe Sean wouldn't support Kiki when Kiki got on Tia's case.

Just before she got to the garage, Tia thought of a way to make Sean a better friend.

Half a block away, she killed the engine, opened the hood, and loosened one of the battery cables. When she got back in the driver's seat and tried to start the van, the battery didn't even click.

"Perfect," she thought. "The van is dead. Now Sean can rescue me. What guy doesn't want to be a hero?"

Five minutes later, Tia spun a tale of woe at the garage about how the minivan had died up the street. Everything worked as she'd planned. Sean and his boss pushed the van to the garage, then set up Tia with water and a magazine, and told her to sit tight.

"I'll figure this out," Sean vowed. "Don't you worry none."

"I know I'm in good hands," Tia had cooed.

Tia realized that she'd just set up an excellent test for Sean.

If he hands me a bunch of bull about something being seriously wrong with the van, I'll know that Kiki's boyfriend is a crook. That's useful. But if he's honest...

"Tia?" Sean lifted his head out from under the hood of the minivan. "Come here. Let me show you what's going on."

"I don't know much about cars," Tia fibbed. "Will it cost a lot to fix?"

Sean shook his head. "I'd like to say yes, but the answer is no. Look here." He pointed to the battery. "Just a loose connection. I tightened 'er up, easy as pie. No charge."

"Oh, thank you!" Tia gushed.

"You're lucky she died where she did," Sean told her.

"I sure am," Tia agreed.

"Now sit down and I'll do that oil change. We'll have you out of here in twenty minutes."

"Thanks, Sean. I really mean it."

Sean wore his coveralls and a matching blue baseball cap. He doffed his cap at Tia. "Always happy to help a beautiful friend."

Tia grinned as she went back to her chair. This was going almost too well.

Sean had promised the oil change would take twenty minutes. He finished in twelve.

"All done!" he reported, handing the keys to Tia.

"That's amazing. You're so good at this."

"Awww ... it's nice to get compli-mented. That'll be twenty-five bucks." Sean fidgeted bashfully.

"Kiki doesn't compliment you?" Tia queried, as she dug around in her pants for some money. She'd come in black jeans, a red T-shirt, and flip-flops. Nothing fancy.

"Not much," Sean admitted. "It's not really her thing."

Tia shook her head. "Too bad. A great guy deserves to hear that he's great. Don't you think?"

Sean shrugged. "That's not for me to say."

"You're modest. Another great thing for a guy to be." Tia held out the cash. "Best twenty-five dollars of my life. Thank you, Sean."

Sean took the money. It felt to Tia like his hand lingered against hers for an instant longer than it needed to.

*Is he interested in me? That would be ...
amazing.*

"Will I see you on Wednesday, when we start building the booths?" she asked.

"Count on it."

"Good," Tia told him. "I wish we could start right now."

Four hours later, Tia and Nishell were at work at the Northeast Towers day-care, supervising the noisy chaos of twenty preschool-age children doing arts and crafts, which really meant smearing chalk and crayons on every surface they could find.

"How long till rest period?" Nishell asked, as one kid launched a crayon at another.

"Thirty-one minutes and eight seconds," Tia told her. "Not that I'm counting."

Nishell fingered the camera that was almost always around her neck. She was not just the official YC photographer, but the day-care's official photographer as well. "I want to thank you for that great idea about the street fair. My photo booth, I mean. YC's gonna make a lotta chip."

Tia's eyes widened. Right then and there, she'd gotten another great idea for her best friend. Nishell would be so grateful when she heard it. "You know, Nishell, I think that booth should be successful for you personally, as well as for YC."

"Whatchu mean by that?" Nishell asked, then cupped her hands by her mouth and yelled at a couple of kids by the far wall. "Malcolm and Toni! You two quit fightin' over the finger paints or you can forget snacks!"

Tia picked up a few stray crayons.

When the kids calmed down, Nishell faced Tia again. "You were sayin'?"

The more Tia thought about her idea, the more excited she got. "Well ... there will be all these people—we hope—coming to get their portraits done by you. Right?"

Nishell nodded.

"The way I see it, every person who comes to the booth should be an advertisement for you. Personally."

"I don't get it," Nishell admitted.

Tia smiled. If Nishell ever developed as good a head for business as she did for taking pictures, she could be rich. "Here's the thing. People are going to go home with portrait photographs, right? You should slide all those pictures into cardboard frames that have your name and address on the back. And have business cards to give out."

Nishell's jaw fell open. "Tia, that's genius!"

"Thank you." Tia was happy to help her friend. It would make her friend want to help her, someday. "Something like, 'Nishell Saunders, photographer.' E-mail address, phone number, like that."

"Who's gonna print these up?"

"I say, let's call Big Boss Printing," Tia said confidently. "Tell him you're with YC. I bet he'll give you a good price. If you don't have the money, I'll front you. Pay me back when you get some clients. We can layout your card and the frame right here on the day-care computer during rest period."

Nishell looked stunned. "How'd you think of all that?"

For a moment, Tia was tempted to tell Nishell more about her life in Nuevo Laredo. A person had to be resourceful there just to survive. Guys building houses would reuse the wood and nails from places that had been abandoned or had fallen down. Tia had gone door to door with her mother's *pan de muerto*, asking neighbors to buy. She'd even learned to shoot rabbits with a slingshot, just so they could have meat.

This wasn't the time for that talk, though. Not with a bunch of screaming kids that they were supposed to be looking after.

"All I know is that Saturday is an opportunity," Tia declared. "You have to make the most of it."

Tia and Nishell got permission to use the day-care computer during rest period. Tia quickly found some templates for photo frames and business cards. They filled them in and sent them to Big Boss's e-mail account. Meanwhile, Nishell called Big Boss. The former Major League Baseball player promised to have the printing done by Friday. Total cost? Thirty-two bucks.

When she got off the phone with Big Boss, Nishell threw her arms around Tia. "I'm lovin' you right now."

Tia beamed. With Sherise and Kiki so down on her, it felt great to be loved by Nishell. If only she could get the rest of YC to feel the same way ...

Whoa.

Tia got another great idea. If this one worked out, the whole YC would love her. Except for Kiki and Sherise. They'd act like they loved her, but they would actually be crazy jealous.

CHAPTER

5

Have a seat over there," the blond receptionist told Tia. "One of Jessica's people will be out in a moment."

"Thank you," Tia said politely. She moved to a small waiting area with a couch and three cushioned chairs. On the opposite wall was a TV monitor showing the morning edition of *Eyewitness Action News*. Tia found herself watching a feature by ace reporter, Jessica Hollander, about fake organic vegetables being sold at a local farmers' market.

Jessica was tall, willowy, and very blond. Her voice was sweet but commanding. Tia could see how she'd become the most popular TV news person in the city. Tia had met her once, when Jessica had come to South Central High School to do a story.

It was the next day, Tuesday, Tia's day off from the day-care. Tia had awakened, worked out, and opened the bakery. At the stroke of nine she put her plan of the day before into action. She called the television station and asked to talk to Jessica Hollander's producer. When the producer answered, she made her pitch. He'd loved the idea, but said Jessica approved her own stories.

Could Tia come talk to Jessica in person?

Tia put on her nicest outfit—black trousers, white silk blouse, and a black vest—and took the bus downtown. She wondered how long she'd have to—

"Tia Ramirez?"

Tia looked up. She'd expected the producer, but there was Jessica herself. Her blond hair was pinned up, and she wore a tight green skirt with a matching white-and-green blouse. She smiled with the confidence of someone who looked good and knew it.

Tia stood. "Hello, Ms. Hollander. I'm Tia Ramirez from South Central—"

"Tia! I remember you!" Jessica told her. She was easily nine inches taller than Tia and wasn't even in heels. "My producer says you have a great segment idea. Why don't you come inside where we can talk?"

Tia nodded, more nervous than she thought she'd be. She followed Jessica through a security door. Just beyond the door was a big room with a long oak table, a dozen chairs, and three TV monitors. Jessica sat, motioning for Tia to join her.

Who do I think I'm kidding? She must get a hundred calls a day. She's never going to want to do this. Why did I ever think—

"So, let's hear it. Quickly. I don't have much time."

Wow. Talk about jumping right in.

Tia took a deep breath. She realized this was another opportunity. She'd created it. She had to make the most of it.

"I'll be brief," Tia promised. "You know our school. It's a tough place, but we had a great yearbook. That yearbook happened because of the girls in the yearbook club. Not that the boys didn't help, but it was mostly us girls."

Jessica's eyes shined with interest. "Girl power. I love that."

"It's definitely a girl-power story," Tia plunged on. "I was thinking that it would be great to follow what the YC—that's yearbook club—girls are doing over the summer before senior year. This is the perfect week, because we've got a big fundraiser planned for the street fair."

"So, a week in the summer life of YC, and we end at the fair on Saturday," Jessica summarized.

"Exactly."

"And this 'YC' asked you to come down here and talk to me," Jessica said, with some admiration in her voice. "That's very smart of everyone."

Tia knew that wasn't exactly true. No one had asked her. No one even knew she was here. She'd come on her own. If she failed, no one would even know about it. But if it worked, she'd be a hero. Everyone would love her, and she'd be elected YC president next year for sure.

That would burn Sherise and Kiki's butts.

"Thank you," Tia said modestly.

Jessica's eyes bored into Tia's. "I'm thinking a two-part feature. Maybe we air it on Thursday or Friday night, then shoot more film at the street fair and do a follow-up early next week."

Omigosh. She's going to do it.

"I'm going to lean on you a lot for this story, Tia," Jessica went on. "We don't have much time. I have a great camera guy, but I'm going to need your help to find the girls, give me background information, all of that."

"I won't let you down," Tia promised. "When do we start?"

"I hope you don't have plans for the rest of the day," the reporter declared. "We start now."

As Tia, Jessica, and her burly cameraman, Paco, approached the door of the Northeast Towers community room, Tia knew that Kiki was in for the shock of her life. Once Tia explained to the TV people that Kiki worked as a tutor with little kids, Jessica suggested that they do an "ambush." An ambush meant her just showing up with a camera crew and asking questions. She said people were more natural when they couldn't prepare.

"This is it," Tia told the news people. The community center door was closed.

"Tia, hang back," Jessica commanded. "I don't want your friend to see you yet."

Friend? I'd never call Kiki a friend. If Kiki wants to be a friend, she has to act like a friend. I never did anything to her except say I wanted to win the scholarship.

Tia took a few steps back. Jessica knocked. A moment later, Kiki opened the door.

Jessica greeted her brightly. "Hi! Kiki Butler?"

"Yeah?" Kiki was stunned, as she took in the reporter and her cameraman.

"I'm Jessica Hollander from *Eyewitness Action News*. We're doing a feature on the girls of South Central High School's yearbook club. Can we visit with you and your tutoring program?"

Kiki—who was wearing jeans and a gray flannel T-shirt with the sleeves cut off, her hair in her usual braids—could barely muster words. "Yeah, I guess—"

"Surprise!" Tia stepped out from behind Jessica. "Big TV story about YC. I'd say 'yes' if I were you."

"You set this up?"

Tia nodded, psyched to see how Kiki was off-balance. "On very short notice. You in or not? It's great publicity, and not just for YC. For your tutoring business, too, you know."

It was a delicious moment as Tia watched Kiki squirm. Kiki knew that Tia had talked to the station without telling anyone. On the other hand, she was smart enough to realize that a TV feature would help both the YC and herself.

"Didn't you know that Tia was setting up this interview?" Jessica asked Kiki.

Kiki brightened, then fibbed baldly. "Of course I knew. I just didn't know it was going to happen this morning. Thanks, Tia, for putting this together. You're the bomb. Really. Ms. Hollander—"

"Jessica," the reporter corrected.

"Jessica, come in," Kiki said, quickly tucking her shirt into her pants. "I'd love for you to meet my students."

For the next half-hour or so, Tia waited quietly while Jessica interviewed Kiki and a couple of the kids that she was tutoring. Jessica asked about how Kiki came up with the idea for the business, how much she charged, how she got her students, and even how people could contact Kiki if they wanted their own kids to get reading lessons.

As Paco filmed, Kiki showed Jessica how her students would sit on plastic milk crates or lay down on donated small rugs.

"I found people to donate kids' books, which are over on that bookcase," Kiki pointed out, in her most teacher-ly voice. "Plus, I charge less for people who can't afford the usual. You can get your kid in a group lesson for an hour for as little as seven bucks. Dollars, I mean. For anyone out there who's interested, that is."

"That's fantastic!" Jessica asked, "Do you like to read yourself, Kiki?"

Kiki nodded. "I love it. Books are the best."

Jessica turned back toward her cameraman and put an arm around Kiki. "True wisdom, spoken by the first of our amazing girls from the South Central High School Yearbook Club. Next stop, the Eastside Mall, to meet Kiki's twin sister, Sherise Butler. This is Jessica Hollander, *Eyewitness Action News.*"

The cameraman's red light went off. Jessica relaxed.

"Okay, that wraps it here," the reporter said. "Tia, you're coming out to the mall with us, right?"

"Right, Jessica!" Tia responded to her with enthusiasm. She wanted Kiki to know that she would be at every interview, in addition to being interviewed herself.

"Excellent. We'll see you in the truck. How about we stop and get a coffee on the way?" Tia thought fast. If Kiki could get free publicity out of this project, why couldn't the bakery?

"Jessica, why don't we stop at my parents' *panadéria* on the way? There's coffee, and the pastries are amazing."

"A *panadéria*? A taste of home. Great idea. Love it!" Paco exclaimed.

Jessica grinned. "When it comes to coffee, Paco's the boss. See you at the truck."

After the TV crew departed for their truck, Kiki came back to where Tia was standing. "Nice one, Tia. Don't think I don't get whatchu did."

Tia decided it was worth one more try to make peace with Kiki.

"Come on, Kiki. I know I set this up without going through you and Sherise, but can you blame me? If I'd suggested it, you would have said no, or you would have wanted credit. I told Jessica she should cover all the girls, not just me. That was the fair thing to do. All you have to do is be fair to me. I can do a lot of good."

Kiki dead-eyed her. "Forget it. I don't trust you, Tia. I'll never trust you. You're only out for yourself."

"That is not true!" Tia said, more hotly than she wanted. She'd tried to make peace with Kiki. Kiki had just thrown it back in her face.

"It is true," Kiki retorted. "Congrats. You win this time. But you won't always win."

"Actually, I will win," Tia told her. She hesitated a moment. "I guess I'll see you and Sean tomorrow, when we're building the booths."

Kiki grimaced. "Don't talk to me 'bout Sean right now."

Tia raised her eyebrows. "What's going on with Sean?"

Kiki scowled. "Nothin' you need to know."

"No problem, then. Well, I better be going. See you tomorrow."

Tia headed for the door. There was trouble in paradise with Sean. Too bad that couldn't go on *Eyewitness Action News*.

CHAPTER

6

The next day was Wednesday. After evening rush hour, the city had closed Twenty-Third Street between King Memorial Drive and Arthur Ashe Boulevard, a distance of about a half mile. Twenty-Third Street was the commercial drag in the hood, but it would stay closed until after the fair. Already the pavement was filled with people from community groups, churches, businesses, and clubs, erecting their booths.

Twenty thousand people were expected. There would be two hundred and fifty booths, as well as a slew of food trucks at the Ashe Boulevard end, selling everything from hot dogs to tacos to soul food. At the King Memorial Drive end, city workers were erecting a big stage. Tone Def would perform; Alicia Keys was rumored to be closing the show. The street fair was big time, and everyone knew it.

The yearbook club crew was taking it seriously. They'd assembled a big team to construct the four booths Tia had suggested: Soak-the-Sap, Basketball Challenge, Nishell's Photo Perfection, and Street Makeovers.

Of all the YC members, Tia had come the most prepared. She'd borrowed her father's tool belt, and she knew how to use everything on it. She'd learned in Mexico and honed her skills helping her parents to remodel the bakery. Everyone was calling for her to help them.

"Tia? Can you bring that drill?"

"Yo, Tia? You got an extra hammer?"

"Hey, Tia! I hear you can handle a hacksaw. Can you cut this for me?"

Jessica Hollander and Paco trailed behind Tia as she headed over to the makeover booth area.

"You seem pretty indispensable with that tool belt, Tia," Jessica observed.

"Just doing my part."

Sean gave Tia a little wave as she passed him. He was helping Jackson and Kiki put together a portable basketball hoop. She waved back.

"I think it's more than that. I'm starting to think you're the most important part of YC," Jessica suggested. "Everyone knows it too."

They reached the makeover booth. Or what would be the makeover booth, once a frame was built, plywood added, and some decent lighting and mirrors installed so Sherise and Marnyke could do their thing.

"We're all important here," Tia said gallantly. "I'm not even the president. That's Sherise. Right, Sherise?"

Sherise had put on a set of white coveralls to do the work; Marnyke was in red overalls with just the thinnest tank top underneath it. Each managed to look fly, even though they were working.

"I can do my *own* nails," Sherise told the reporter. "But I can't do the kind of nails that will put this booth together." Everyone laughed.

"Me neither," Marnyke chimed in. "That makes Tia real important."

"Just doing my part," Tia said, as she expertly drilled some holes, then fastened them with long screws and clamped the two-by-fours together for extra strength. "Watch what I'm doing, chicas. Then you can do it too."

Sherise and Marnyke shared a skeptical look, but listened carefully as Tia gave them a quick but useful lesson in how to construct the booth frame.

"Thanks, Tia," Sherise said.

Whoa. Did Sherise just say thank you to me? It has to be because the camera is rolling.

"You're welcome, you guys," she told them, then turned to the reporter. "You see, Jessica? That's how we YC girls support each other."

"I see," said Jessica. Then the reporter moved to Marnyke. "You're Marnyke Cooper, right? I haven't interviewed you for the story yet."

"That's me, yup," Marnyke said. She seemed a little nervous to be on camera, especially in front of Tia. So nervous, in fact, that as she tried to nail together a couple of two-by-fours, she bent the nail into a U shape.

"Tell me about yourself," Jessica prompted.

"Not much to tell," Marnyke muttered.

"Oh, don't be modest," Jessica went on. "You YC girls are all outstanding in your own ways. What are you great at, Marnyke?"

Tia could think of a snarky answer to that question, but kept her mouth shut.

Lattrell, who happened to be passing by with shopping bags full of bottled waters for the crew, had no such self-control. "What she good at? She good at gettin' the boys!"

Jessica's questioning turned sharp. "Is that true, Marnyke? Is that your best skill?"

Marnyke stood frozen, grasping the hammer for dear life.

Rescue her. Rescue her now.

Tia stepped between Marnyke and the reporter. "Umm ... Jessica? Marnyke here is the one person who keeps this whole club together. She's like ... the YC glue."

"Is that so?" Jessica asked.

"Totally," Tia declared. "At prom this year? We were a mess. I mean, we worked so hard on the yearbook that except for Sherise, none of us knew what to wear. Marnyke hooked us up with prom dresses and got us the makeovers that were the inspiration for this very booth!"

"Is that true?" Jessica asked Marnyke.

"I don't—well, kinda, yeah," Marnyke murmured, looking at Tia in wonder and gratitude.

"Marnyke doesn't like to brag," Tia added. "But she could make a cactus look hot!"

Jessica laughed. So did Paco and Marnyke.

That wasn't hard. Marnyke's in my bag now.

"Well then," Jessica said. "If that's the case, I might have to stop by on Saturday for a makeover myself!"

Everyone laughed again. Then the reporter and her cameraman moved off toward the stage that was under construction.

Marnyke came over to give her a hug.

"Nice one," Sherise told Tia.

"Thanks, I—"

They were interrupted by the sound of an argument over by the basketball hoop. Kiki and Sean were in each other's faces.

"Is that the way you feel, Kiki? Is that why you treat me that way?" Sean challenged.

"I feel how I feel, and nothing's changing!" Kiki fired back.

" 'Cause you take me for granted, you know. Like you know I'm gonna be here. 'Good ol' Sean. He don't make no trouble.

So why should I pay him any mind at all?' " Sean's voice got nasty.

Kiki got furious. "You know what, Sean King? I don't need you. I don't want you, and I don't have to have you. If I never see you again? That's too soon for me!"

With that, Kiki stormed off. Tia saw the looks of shock on everyone's faces. She did her best to look shocked too.

What she was really feeling, though, was happiness. The worse things got between Kiki and Sean, the better things would be for Tia. If only there was a way to make it last into the school year, so Kiki could get distracted from her schoolwork.

Sean stomped away toward the Ashe Boulevard end of the street. After a discreet few minutes, Tia took a chance and followed. It wasn't hard to catch up; he'd stopped to sit on some benches near a booth that was being erected by a crew from a local church.

"Hey," she said.

"Hey."

"I saw you and Kiki before. I'm sorry."

Sean shrugged. "I'm not. Better to get it out in the open. She was wastin' my time, anyway."

"Good. Then you're not too upset?"

He smiled warmly. "Nah. How upset can I be when I got the beautiful Bionic Latina talking to me?"

Tia blushed despite herself. She'd never heard the nickname used so warmly. "I don't know," she said. "How upset could you be?"

"So upset that what I really want to do is ask you out," he declared. "Tomorrow, Kiki and I were going out with Marnyke and her guy, Gabe. Maybe go race one of his daddy's sports cars in Majestic Oaks.

I was wondering—how would you like to do that with me instead?"

"Take Kiki's place, you mean?" Tia hesitated. "Won't that be weird?"

"Yes—no—well ..."

"Okay." Tia put Sean out of his misery. "I'd love to."

"Yeah?" Sean's face lit up.

Just like that, it was a date. Tia couldn't wait to hear what Kiki had to say about it.

She didn't have to wait long. Three hours later, she was home and getting ready for bed when the text came in from Kiki.

My man messin' with u? U can have him!

CHAPTER

7

Fourth gear, *now*," Sean shouted over the roar of the red Ferrari Testarossa's 390-horsepower engine, as it roared onto the half-mile back straightaway of the road course at the private Majestic Oaks Auto Club track.

Tia was already in fourth. As she shifted into fifth and jammed her foot on the gas, the Ferrari shot forward like a jet fighter with afterburners ignited. One hundred twenty miles an hour. One twenty-five. One thirty. One forty!

"Go, girl!" Sean encouraged.

"Hold on!" Tia warned, as a sharp S-curve loomed. She downshifted without braking; the revolutions-per-minute gauge on the dashboard jumped toward the red zone. The car swung through the two sharp curves, G-forces pushing Tia and Sean into their seats. Tia accelerated out and zoomed into a short straight section that led to a sweeping right-hand curve, and then the final straightaway to the start/finish line.

She crossed that line at a hundred and forty-three miles an hour. There was an automatic timer that displayed both her miles per hour and lap time for the two mile track: she'd covered it in a minute and two seconds.

"Damn, girl!" Sean exclaimed. "You ready for the Indy 500!"

Tia rolled the Ferrari into the pits, where Marnyke and Gabe were waiting near a vintage Chaparral racing car from the 1960s.

"Where'd you learn to drive like that?" Sean demanded.

"Mexico." Tia shrugged. She pulled the Ferrari up next to the Chaparral and killed the engine.

"I'm serious," Sean declared.

She unfastened the shoulder harness and took off the black crash helmet Gabe had given her. "It's true. Everyone in Mexico knows how to drive a standard."

"But you've never raced a car before?"

Tia shook her head. "Nope. But I want to do it again!"

That is the understatement of the year. I loved it so much. One day, I'm going to own a car like this. I'm going to earn it with my own blood, sweat, and tears. I won't need a man to give it to me. Look at Marnyke. She's staring at Gabe like he's a blank check to the World Bank. What

*if he drops her? She's out of luck. No way.
I'm going to take care of myself.*

It was the next evening. The day had
been long—Tia had gone from the bakery
to the day-care to Twenty-Third Street,
where she'd done more work on booths.
Everything was setting up perfectly.

She and Sean had worked on the
Soak-the-Sap booth and figured out the
rules of the game. They decided that
each contestant would pay a dollar and
get three baseballs. If the contestant
could throw any of the baseballs through
a hole in a target twenty-five feet away,
the operator would pull back on a platform support. Then the sap on the platform would tumble five feet into a deep
pool filled with ice water.

The only question was, who would be
the sap?

Right before they'd come out here
to Majestic Oaks, Tia had worked the

phones, asking people to take a half-hour shift. So far, she'd convinced a city council member to take a turn, as well as Mr. Olson, the school principal. She'd even called Mr. Crandall, the hated guidance counselor, but he'd begged off, claiming a head cold.

"Right," Tia had thought. "He just doesn't want a line of people all waiting to soak him."

The best part was that everyone seemed to accept that Sean and Kiki were over, and that Sean and Tia were together. Marnyke said how much she was looking forward to hanging with Sean and Tia. Even Sherise said she thought Tia was a better match for Sean than her sister.

As for Kiki, she didn't even show up to work on the booths. Tia figured she was too upset.

Before they'd come over to the track, Tia, Sean, Gabe, and Marnyke had hung out at the Olympic-size pool at Gabe's father's place. Tia had been shocked by the size of the estate. Gabe lived in one of the guesthouses; he had two bedrooms and zero parents looking over his shoulder. Though he said he wasn't interested in money, Tia could tell he didn't mind taking advantage of the toys that were available to him. Like these sports cars.

That Marnyke loved the toys was obvious from the way she hung onto Gabe's sleeve for dear life.

"You drive that thing like you own it, Tia," Gabe observed. His brown curly hair was tousled; he had a couple of days' growth of beard. Tia found him hot, in a scruffy musician kind of way.

"Thanks," Tia told him.

"Kiki never drove like that," Gabe commented. "Kiki never drove out here at all."

"Let's leave Kiki out of this, okay?" Sean suggested. "Tia is more than enough girl for me."

"Fair enough," Gabe agreed. "You guys want to head back to my place to, um, hang out?"

Tia knew what "hang out" meant. It was code for "hittin' it."

What's Sean going to say? Because there's no way I want to have—

Sean shook his head. "You guys go and have fun. Tia and I are gonna get to know each other a little bit better 'fore we get to that. If we get to that."

My hero. I may be the last virgin at South Central High School, but I'm going to stay that way. No way I'm messing up my life with a baby. Accidents can happen!

Marnyke grinned. "You guys do that. You gonna like her a lot."

Sean smiled. "I already like her a lot."

I already like him a lot too. This was supposed to be kind of a joke, me getting close to Sean. But maybe it could turn out to be a whole lot more.

"I didn't know this place existed!" Tia exclaimed, as Sean pulled into a small gravel parking lot and turned off the engine of his old Ford Taurus.

"Not many do," Sean told her. "You kinda have to know your way in. It's a nice night. Let's sit on the roof."

It was forty-five minutes later. Sean had driven them back to the city. While they were on the road, the sky had grown starry. Tia had thought that maybe they'd end up at Mio's Pizzeria, but instead, Sean had taken them to the other side of town and then up a winding dirt road to a hilltop dotted with huge television, radio, and microwave relay towers. They weren't really all that high, but it was the tallest spot near the city and the view was incredible.

"It's beautiful," Tia breathed, taking in the expanse of lights below and the moon and stars above.

"Not as beautiful as the girl I'm with," Sean told her.

"Come on!" Tia chided. "I'm still in day-care clothes."

"You did a hundred forty-five miles an hour in those day-care clothes," Sean said with a laugh. "Meanwhile, I got car grease under my nails."

"I don't care," Tia said.

A helicopter passed overhead; they waited for the whir of the chopper blades to fade into the distance before they said anything else.

"What do you care about?" Sean asked quietly.

"My family," Tia answered quickly. "I care about my family. They've taken care of me and brought me here to America. I want to be the American dream for them."

"How do you go about doin' that?" He turned and looked at her with such open and welcoming eyes that she felt completely comfortable confiding in him.

"I can tell you the truth?" she asked.

"If it isn't the truth, what's it worth?" he wondered aloud.

A few fireflies flitted in the distance, forming moving constellations as striking as the stars above. Tia watched in wonder and decided they were another sign that she could trust the boy she was with.

"Here's the truth. I won't cheat, unless people cheat me. I will be nice to people that I don't like if I have to, if it helps me. And I can't stand most of the YC kids because they're either lazy, out for themselves, or don't play fair. Marnyke's a parasite with that rich white guy. Kiki? She's ugly inside and out. Sherise is as two-faced as they come. And that's just the girls. The guys are just as bad, if not worse."

"Are you going to do anything about it?" Sean asked.

"Absolutely. They'll never know how I really feel, that's for sure. I'm going to keep doing things that look good for everyone but are actually best for me. I got that TV lady to do the story about us, right? No one will ever know what I really think. And to me, that's the best part of all."

She looked at Sean and realized that she was lucky the YC kids hadn't heard that. They'd hate her guts. On the other hand, it felt good to share her feelings with someone.

"Please don't tell anyone," she added quickly.

Sean smiled. "Who would I tell? What would I tell? That you use people? Everybody uses people. At least you bein' honest about it."

"Do you ever use people?"

"Who doesn't?" He picked up her hand and kissed it gently. "Until we get to know each other better."

Tia had been kissed before. Ty and she had done some serious kissing, in fact. But she thought that nothing had ever felt better than Sean's lips on the back of her small hand.

"Um, can you do that again?" she whispered.

He did.

CHAPTER
8

It was late Friday afternoon. Up and down Twenty-Third Street, hundreds of people were putting the finishing touches on their booths. Mrs. Phillips had let Tia and Nishell leave the day-care early so they could pitch in at the YC booths.

For the last three hours, Tia had worked harder than anyone else. She was everywhere, scraping, sanding, painting, and repainting. She went so far as to get on her knees with a spatula and a bottle of solvent to get gum wads off the street so they wouldn't stick to people's shoes in the hot weather.

Jessica and the camera crew had filmed that, too, before heading down to the studio to finish their segment. It would air that night on the evening edition of *Eyewitness Action News*. The whole YC was going to watch together at Mio's Pizzeria. Even though Twenty-Third Street was closed to auto traffic, Mio's stayed open.

Before they could head over, though, the booth captains each gave a short speech on how things would work the next day. Sherise talked about the make-over booth. Nishell explained the photo area. Jackson and Carlos showed people how the basketball challenge would be done. Finally, the YC kids gathered around Tia as she walked them through Soak-the-Sap.

"This pool is fifteen by fifteen," Tia declared. "As you can see, it's already filled with water."

"Ain't it supposed to be ice water?" Jackson called out.

"It is," Tia agreed. "We'll dump in a hundred pounds every hour on the half-hour. To the left will be the cashier. To the right, the play area itself. We'll work in groups of three. For example, Jackson could be on cash, I'll supervise the play, and we'll put Carlos on the platform. I bet he hopes no one soaks him."

"Don't let Jackson nowhere near the cash, Tia," Lattrell hooted. "You'll never see it again!"

The kids cracked up. Tia grinned. It seemed like she was the real leader of YC now. Sherise might be president, but she was boss.

Kiki raised her hand. "Tia?"

Tia was surprised that Kiki had even shown up. Kiki and Sean hadn't said more than a curt "hello" to each other.

"Yes, Kiki?"

"Have you thought about who's going to take care of the money during the fair? I mean, from all the booths? I'm worried about that."

Ha. This is great. Kiki's the yearbook manager, but she's asking me how things are going to work.

Tia *had* thought about that, and in fact had contacted Ms. Okoro. "I'm glad you asked," she said politely. "I e-mailed Ms. Okoro. She'll be back from San Francisco in the morning. She said she'll hold it for us."

"You think of everything," Kiki said approvingly.

"I try to," Tia told her, wondering whether to trust Kiki's new attitude or not. She looked out over her classmates. "Any more questions?"

There were none.

"Well then," she said, getting excited despite herself, "there's just one more thing to do. Let's go to Mio's and watch ourselves on TV!"

To Tia's surprise, Mio's was jammed. Not just with kids in YC, but with parents, friends, and lots of people from school who'd heard about the broadcast. Right off the bat, Tia spotted the Butler twins' parents, Mrs. Phillips from the day-care, and a bunch of day-care counselors. There were players from the various school teams, plus kids Tia had seen hanging with Carlos, Jackson, and Lattrell, but had never met. Even Marnyke's white boyfriend had showed up.

"If only my mother and father were here," Tia thought wistfully. "But they're working. They'd be so proud. Ms. O too."

Sean stepped over to her. "Hungry?"

She pointed to the counter. People stood five-deep, calling out orders to the boss. "No way we're getting through that!"

Sean laughed. "I figured the Bionic Latina could just snap her fingers and make a slice appear. Or the crowd would part for the YC diva. Kinda like the Red Sea for Moses."

Tia waved a finger at him. "Very funny."

"Maybe after this we can go someplace a little quieter?" Sean asked.

Tia smiled. "I'd like that."

"Me too."

Mio's had two wall-mounted screens that were usually tuned to sports. Tonight, though, they'd show the news. Tia wondered how anyone could hear. The noise level from the crowd was that loud.

She didn't have to wait long for her answer. As a graphic for "Remarkable

Girls!" flashed on the monitors, people shouted for quiet. An instant later, Mio's was as still as a library at midnight, with all eyes on the televisions.

"Prepare to feel good about the future," said the handsome white anchorman. "Here's *Eyewitness Action News* award-winning reporter Jessica Hollander with the first of a special two-part segment on some unforgettable girls everyone should know about."

Tia's heart raced as the scene shifted to Jessica standing outside the locked front door of the high school.

"South Central High School," she intoned. "Everyone knows its reputation. The leaky ceiling and crumbling walls. The poor test scores. The drugs and gang violence."

The scene shifted to a close-up of the high school yearbook. "Yet with all these challenges, a group of outstanding girls are on a mission to change your minds about their school. Come meet the girls of the South Central High School Yearbook Club!"

The crowd in Mio's cheered as the scene shifted to Kiki at her tutoring business. A brief chant of "Kiki, Kiki!" started, then people shushed each other to listen. Jessica showed a few moments of Kiki at work, and then a chunk of her interview with Kiki that made Kiki seem like some kind of a hero.

From Kiki, Jessica worked her way through the rest of the YC girls. Sherise, at the clothing store where she worked. Then Nishell, taking photographs at the day-care. Then Marnyke, whom Jessica described as "modest about her sartorial and maquillage talents," whatever that meant.

"What about you?" Sean whispered to Tia.

Suddenly, the camera focused on a yearbook picture of Tia. Jessica narrated.

"Perhaps the most remarkable of this group of girls is the one who has emerged as their unofficial leader, cheerleader, and go-to person for problems large and small."

The images shifted to Tia at the street fair using a hand drill, then teaching Sherise and Marnyke how to nail together two-by-fours.

"You look good in a tool belt," Sean murmured.

Jessica's narration continued. "Two years ago, Tia Ramirez and her family lived in Nuevo Laredo, Mexico, where bodies of those killed in drug-related violence are found on the streets every morning. Now, they're here as legal immigrants. Tia's parents work brutal hours, running a Mexican bakery where

I can tell you the pastries are quite wonderful."

Here, the scene shifted to the exterior of the bakery, and then the display case inside from when they'd detoured there for coffee. Tia was thrilled; this would be great for business.

The scene shifted again, back to Tia at the fair. She and Nishell were side by side, painting the photo booth. "Eighteen months ago, Tia barely spoke English. Now she's one of the two top students at South Central High School. I can tell you that this is one of the most capable young women you will ever hope to meet."

Someone shouted, "Go, Tia!"

Tia barely heard from the blood pounding in her ears. There she was, on American television, for all to see.

Jessica still wasn't done. "On Saturday, Tia and the other YC girls, as they call themselves, will have several booths at the Twenty-Third Street Fair. Our team will be there to capture the fun. Come and support these remarkable young people!"

The report ended; the Mio's crowd erupted into whoops, hollers, and cheering. People that Tia knew and people that she didn't came over to clap her on her back. She spotted Kiki alone across the room. Kiki gave a thumbs-up. Tia flashed one right back at her.

If only my mom and dad could have—

Tia heard someone calling in Spanish from near the counter.

"*Hija! Hija mia!* My daughter!"

It was her mother. Somehow, she'd made it to Mio's for the broadcast, and Tia hadn't seen her in the crush. Her heart brimming with love, Tia pushed through the crowd to where her mother stood with open arms. She hugged her mom tight, surprised and happy.

"I'm so proud of you, *hija*," her mother said.

"Thank you. Thank you for everything, Mama," Tia murmured.

She meant every single word.

CHAPTER

9

Yo, Tone! Yo! Right over here! These be the kids you wanna meet. Over here!" Tone Def's manager—an older African American man in the flowing saffron-colored robes of a North African tribesman—called to the world-famous hip-hop star.

Tone Def was a legend in the city, having come from these mean streets to gain stardom. For today's street fair, he wore a white linen suit with a white bowler hat that would have looked stupid-ass on anyone else. By the time he was done with his show, everybody knew the jacket and bowler would be tossed into the adoring crowd—probably his white shoes too.

Tia wasn't a die-hard fan, but it was hard to stay calm as the star, his manager, and three massive bodyguards pushed through the crowd. Tone Def wanted to meet the YC girls before the fair started. Incredible.

The girls—the manager had specified just the girls, so the guys had to hang back—gathered in a semicircle. Tone Def marched up to them.

"Wanna give you girls props," he muttered in his famous gravelly voice. "Saw all ya'll on the tube las' night. 'Nuff respect."

Sherise, as president, spoke for the group. "We're so proud that you'd—"

Tone Def cut her off. "Nah, I wanna talk to that chick with the tool belt. That look like her," he nodded in Tia's direction.

Tia stepped forward. She'd worn a sleeveless black dress for the day, because she expected a lot of people might want to meet her, and she wanted to look good. Plus, Jessica would be filming more. Too bad she was missing this moment.

"I'm Tia Ramirez."

Tone Def offered Tia his hand. Tia took it. The others looked on.

"You the real deal," Tone Def told her, still holding Tia's hand. He looked at the other girls. "This girl be the real deal. Ya'll listen to her. Peace out."

The star turned and headed toward the stage. His bodyguards and manager followed. Meanwhile, the whole YC zoomed toward Tia.

"Omigod, Tia, he held your hand!"

"He wanted to meet you! Just you!"

"Thank you, Tia. Thank you! That was the greatest thing I've ever seen!"

The compliments came from everyone, including Sherise and Kiki. Once again, Tia wondered if she could trust them. Ms. Okoro, who'd come back from vacation in time for the fair, stepped forward. She wore an orange and black outfit from her native Nigeria.

"Okay, everybody," their advisor said. "You've done such wonderful work here, and you've done it on your own. I am so proud of you. Five minutes till they cut the ribbons and start the fair. I think you should get into position."

The gathering broke up. Sean and Tia were going to do the first shift at Soak-the-Sap. Tia would take money, Sean would run the game, and a local DJ named Deadrat would be up on the platform. Tia hoped that Deadrat had a lot of enemies. She wanted her booth to make more money than all the others combined.

Sean took Tia's hand. "Did you know Tone Def was gonna do that?"

Tia shook her head. "No clue. I can get almost anyone to do what I want. Even that television reporter. Before the year is over, I bet I can get her to do another feature just on me. And the rest of YC? They'll be treating me like I'm the queen and they're my serfs."

Sean laughed. "You a diva, all right. Let's go get this party started."

They went over to the booth, dumped ice into the pool, and showed Deadrat—a huge guy in tiny swim trunks—how to get up to the platform. He wasn't there a minute before a cannon boomed to start the fair. People streamed onto Twenty-Third Street.

"Here we go!" Sean called.

Tia grinned. The fair was starting. Everything was under control, and Tone

Def had just told the rest of YC to listen to her.

What could be better than this?

With just forty-five minutes to go before the fair was over, the booths were still raking in money.

The guys on the basketball court were taking on all comers. Nishell had taken so many portraits that she was close to running out of frames. Marnyke and Sherise had used up almost all their makeup supplies. Over at Soak-the-Sap, Tia had given six hundred and fifty dollars to Ms. Okoro for safekeeping. Meanwhile, she was scheduled to do the last half-hour on the platform. Wisely, she'd brought a change of clothes and a towel.

"Gotta think of everything," she mused, as she walked alone up the center line of Twenty-Third Street, taking in the fair's sights and sounds. The streets were still jammed with people of every race and color. A light breeze sent delicious aromas from the food trucks wafting over the crowd. Alicia Keys was the final performer; she'd opened with "Fallin'," and segued into "Empire State of Mind." A mass of people near the stage cheered for her.

It was the weirdest thing. Right here at the fair, maybe for the very first time since her family had come to America, Tia felt almost like she was at home.

That thought made her feel good as she headed back to the booth. Sherise was taking a break from makeup to handle money, while Lattrell was supervising the baseball throwers. On the platform was the principal, Mr. Olson. He'd been a good sport and come to the fair in a three-piece suit. So far, he'd stayed dry.

"I'll go up there now, Mr. Olson!" Tia announced. She wanted to give the principal a break. As small a gesture as it was, she knew it also might help her stay on his good side.

"I'm fine, Tia," Mr. Olson told her.

"Really, I'm ready," Tia insisted.

"If you insist! I like being dry, thank you very much."

A moment later, Mr. Olson had climbed down. He shook Tia's hand. "I hear you had a lot to do with that TV story," he told her quietly. "It made our school look good. I won't forget that. Thank you."

"You're welcome, sir," Tia said.

She said good-bye, then started up the ladder to the platform. From the platform itself—five feet felt really high, and she could see ice cubes bobbing in the water—she spotted Jessica Hollander and her cameraman, Paco, hurrying toward the pool. So did the rest of the YC kids.

"Well, you are a celebrity target," Tia thought wryly.

The first contestant paid her money and lined up to take a throw. It was Kiki. Her face was as grim and focused as if she was pitching against Albert Pujols and the World Series was on the line.

"Shouldn't you be working a booth?" Tia called out. She wasn't really surprised that Kiki was here, considering the way things had been going between them.

"Yeah, I should," Kiki admitted, as she took a baseball pitcher's windup and let fly with the ball at the hole in the plywood now twenty yards away. "But I'm not."

The ball went right through the hole. *Oh no!*

Tia crashed down with a huge belly-flop.

"Yeow!" she yelped as she splashed in the ice-cold water.

Everyone was laughing as she got her bearings, pushed over to the small ladder that would take her out of the pool, climbed out, and looked for a towel. Water sheeted off her soaked dress and body and drenched the pavement. She was glad she'd worn a sports bra and old-lady underwear. Otherwise, she knew she'd look like a contestant in a wet T-shirt contest.

"I'm not done," Kiki announced.

"Huh?" Tia looked up.

"I paid money for three throws. I'm taking them."

"You can't do more than one throw."

Sherise marched over to Tia. "Where does it say that in the rules?"

It was true. There was no rule that said if a person made a successful throw, they were done for the day.

"Okay, okay," Tia admitted and then did the only thing she could to save face. That is, climb up the ladder, get back on the platform, and pray that Kiki's next two throws missed.

Tia's prayers were not answered. Kiki's next toss was perfect.

Splash!

Tia got dunked a second time.

"At least she's only got one more throw," Tia thought. She clambered out of the pool. It was embarrassing to have Jessica Hollander and Paco there, filming her, but she tried to be a good sport about it.

"Maybe you should go out for baseball," she told Kiki.

"Maybe you should get back on the platform," Kiki retorted.

Kiki wound up and threw. *Splash-down!*

Everyone cracked up again at the sight of Tia getting drenched.

Tia got out of the pool one more time, glad that Kiki's turn was done. But as she climbed back up, she saw that trouble was coming. Kiki handed a hundred dollar bill to Sherise, who was taking money for the booth. "This is to pay for anyone who wants a shot at the diva," she announced. "Come one, come all!"

To Tia's shock and surprise, every single kid from YC lined up by where Lattrell was handing out the baseballs. Marnyke. Sherise. Jackson. Even Nishell. None of them was smiling, either. Each was as grim as Kiki had been when she first stepped up to the line.

Something bad was happening. The whole YC had turned against her. But she couldn't really complain since the TV cameras were rolling.

Then Sean pushed to the front of the line.

"I'm next," he told Lattrell. "Gimme the damn ball."

"Sean?" Tia asked in a small voice. "You?"

His answer was to wind up and fire. *Strike!*

Tia splashed down.

CHAPTER

10

S he stood chest-deep in the middle of the pool, her black dress clinging to her body in the cold water. That the whole YC was against her was obvious from the angry faces circling the pool. She looked to see if Ms. Okoro would rescue her, but the club advisor was nowhere in sight. This was no surprise. The advisor liked to let the kids settle their own problems.

Tia met Sean's eyes. This was not the guy she'd come to know. This was someone else, behind a mask of fury. Same with Marnyke. Carlos. Jackson.

Even Nishell was glaring like she was the worst person in the world.

Why is this happening?

Finally, seven o'clock arrived. The fair was over. Tia sloshed through the water and climbed out. No one threw her a towel. Instead, the kids formed a tight circle around her.

"What's going on?" Tia asked. "Is this some kind of joke?"

"Ha!" Kiki barked. "If this be a joke, it be on you!"

"That's for sure," Sean added.

Tia saw Jessica Hollander and her cameraman trying to film all this, but Sherise marched over to her. "Excuse us, Ms. Hollander. This be private."

"Hardly. I'd call it big news," Jessica retorted.

"Carlos? Jackson? Lattrell?" Sherise asserted herself. "Can you keep Ms. Hollander away while we talk to Tia?

Tia, we need you to step into the makeup booth? *Now*."

Except for Sean, all the guys peeled off to block the TV people. Tia, meanwhile, trudged over to the booth where Marnyke and Sherise had been doing their makeovers. She still had neither a towel nor shoes.

Once inside, she turned around. She was surprised to find herself just with Kiki, Sean, and Sherise. All the others, even Nishell, had stayed outside.

Kiki spoke first. "How can you even look at yourself in the mirror?"

Tia held her ground. "I don't know what you're talking about."

"I don't know what you're talking about," Sherise mimicked coldly.

"I mean it. What did I do? Besides make this fair great for everyone?"

The fact was, she'd done plenty to play with people's emotions, to manipulate them into doing what was best for her. She knew that. But there was no way that the kids in YC could know that. She'd been too smart and too careful.

Sean spoke up. "You thought I was this dumb mechanic. You thought I was all into you. You want to see who I'm really into?"

Tia got a sinking feeling in her stomach as Kiki approached Sean. He put his arms around her. She put her arms around him. Then they kissed. It was a long, lingering, get-a-room-you-two kiss that Tia could not look away from even though she tried. Tia grasped at the edge of a table as her knees started to buckle.

Oh. My. God. Sean and Kiki are still together. And I told him everything.

"I love you," Sean said to Kiki.

"I love you, Sean."

Suddenly, Kiki whirled at Tia. "Tee-yuh, you busted! You really think that

Sean would turn on me? I know everything you ever said to him. So does
everyone else in YC!"

Tia felt awful. All this time, Sean and
Kiki had been playing her. They'd set her
up and knocked her down.

Maybe there was a way out of this.
After all, it was just Sean's word against
hers.

"Whatever Sean told you I said?" Tia
declared with dignity. "He's making it up."

Sean smiled. "I don't think so."

He whipped out his cell phone and
pressed a button. To Tia's shock, her own
words from a few nights before, when she
and Sean had been together on the hill
overlooking the city, came back to her.

*Here's the truth. I won't cheat, unless
people cheat me. I will be nice to people
that I don't like if I have to, if it helps
me. And I can't stand most of the YC
kids because they're either lazy, out for*

themselves, or don't play fair. Marnyke's a parasite with that rich white guy. Kiki? She's ugly inside and out. Sherise is as two-faced as they come. And that's just the girls. The guys are just as bad, if not worse.

Tia swallowed hard, but her mouth had gone dry. Sean had taped her, and she'd had no idea. She was in so much trouble. Not just with Kiki and Sherise, but with the rest of the YC kids too. Was there any way to defend herself?

She decided to turn it into a joke. "Oh, come on, guys. You call me the Bionic Latina. So I use people to get what I want. Everyone does. Look at Marnyke and Gabe. That's life."

Kiki shrugged. "Really? If I were you, I'd be scared of a certain someone hearing this. Sean?"

Sean pressed another button on his cell. Tia heard herself one more time, this time from just before the fair started.

Again, she was talking to Sean. Again, he'd secretly recorded her.

I can get almost anyone to do what I want. Even that television reporter. Before the year is over, I bet I can get her to do another feature just on me. And the rest of YC? They'll be treating me like I'm the queen and they're my serfs.

Tia froze. A wave of nausea rolled up her spine to her temples and then back down again to the pit of her stomach. She realized that if Jessica Hollander ever heard that, she was toast. She'd be ruined. The reporter would do a feature about Tia, yes. But it would be about what a terrible, selfish bee-yotch she was. What college would take her after a feature like that was on the air?

"What—what are you going to do with that?" Tia's voice was shaky.

Kiki stared at Tia a long time before she spoke. "I'm not sure. I still gotta decide." She motioned toward Sean's cell. "There's copies of everything. Don't even think about grabbing the phone and throwing it in the pool."

"I wouldn't do that!" Tia protested.

"Why should we believe you?" Sherise asked. "You'd do anything to help yourself."

Tia didn't want to cry but felt tears leak from her eyes.

"Tomorrow," Kiki said softly. "We'll let you know tomorrow what we gonna do. Come on, we outta here."

When the others were gone, Tia found a seat in the booth and collapsed, burying her face in her hands. There was no doubt that she was in deep *mierda*. Worst of all, it was all of her own doing.

CHAPTER

11

The next morning was Sunday. It was all Tia could do to drag herself out of bed and go open the bakery. She moved so slowly that her mom thought she was sick.

She lied and claimed she was fine, but she was nothing close to fine. She was scared. What would happen now? What were the YC kids going to do? Had they already gone to Jessica Hollander? Would the reporter and Paco make an ambush visit to the bakery this very morning: filming, firing questions, and turning Tia into the center of a feature that would make her look like Public Enemy Number One?

The bakery opened at seven on Sundays. The first half hour was the usual rush. She was grateful for the distraction but fearful that Jessica Hollander might show up. By a quarter to eight, though, the place was quiet.

Then the front door bells chimed. Tia's heart sank ... until she saw who was coming in.

It wasn't the reporter. It was the yearbook advisor, Ms. Okoro. Instead of the colorful African clothes she always wore to school, Ms. O looked like a regular person this early on a Sunday morning, in blue sweats and no makeup.

Ms. O was no-nonsense. "Tia, I know all about what happened yesterday. Kiki, Nishell, and Sean are on their way here. We need to talk."

Tia nodded. She admired Ms. Okoro, who was a great teacher. She always felt a bond with her too. Like Tia, Ms. O knew what it was like to be a stranger in a strange land.

"I'm sorry about what happened," Tia said contritely.

"That may be true, but were you sorry before the kids caught you?" Ms. Okoro asked immediately. Then she softened. "Sit, Tia."

"Can I bring you some coffee and churros?" Tia asked.

"That would be lovely," Ms. O said with grace.

Ms. Okoro sat at the table closest to the window while Tia prepared a plate of churros and two cups of coffee. A moment later, she was sitting across from her beloved teacher, who took a churro, dunked it in the coffee, and nibbled it thoughtfully.

—

"I go out of town for one week and look what happens." Ms. O sighed. "One week! I come back; you and Kiki are at war. Do you know how most wars end?"

"With one side winning?" Tia ventured.

Ms. Okoro shook her head. "No, Tia. I saw war in Nigeria. You saw it where you grew up in Mexico. No matter who wins, there are many dead bodies in the street."

"Kiki started it!" Tia defended herself.

"There's a Nigerian proverb that goes like this: 'If one imitates the upright, one becomes upright; if one imitates the crooked, one becomes crooked.' You and Kiki, you have both become crooked," Ms. O declared. "It makes me sick in my heart."

Tia felt awful that her favorite teacher was disappointed in her.

"Are you ready to imitate the upright?" Ms. O asked. "I am not saying, don't compete with Kiki. I am saying to do it fairly."

"I can do that. But if I do it and Kiki doesn't, I'll get hurt all over again."

"Let's see if she will." Ms. O took out her cell and made a quick call. "I'm ready for you in the bakery. Tia is here."

A moment later, Kiki, Sean, and Nishell stepped into the shop. Ms. O motioned them over. Kiki and Sean were dressed for church. Nishell was in shorts and a T-shirt. Tia wondered why Nishell had come instead of Sherise.

"I've spoken to Tia," Ms. O stated. "Does anyone have anything they want to say?"

To Tia's surprise, Nishell was the first one to talk. "For a smart girl who I thought was my friend, you pretty stupid," she said.

"She not so smart, Nishell. Sherise smarter than her." Kiki's voice rose as she turned to Tia. "It was Sherise's idea to make Sean be a spy. Tape you. All that."

"You're kidding," Tia said without thinking. "Sherise came up with that?"

Kiki nodded. "Yep. My sister. Maybe she's not book smart, but she's street smart. Not like you."

"You be street dumb," Sean added.

Ms. O turned to Kiki and Sean. She was furious. "You two are in no position to be calling anyone names. You've acted like children. Setting her up like you did, making fun of her like you did. And you, Sean? Acting like you wanted to be her friend just to hurt her? Taping her words! You could have put a stop to it at any time. Tia is the most valuable person on the yearbook. I am not saying that to defend her. I am stating a fact. Tia will succeed wherever she goes. Do you want her to quit and go to the school newspaper? Or to student council? Do you want to do the yearbook without her?"

Tia was astonished that Ms. Okoro was defending her. Someone was paying attention.

Kiki looked down at the tabletop. "No," she muttered.

"Then be a real leader." Ms. Okoro slid her eyes over to Tia. "And you? We've talked already. You need to play fair. Treat people like you want to be treated. Don't use people, if you don't want to be used."

Ms. Okoro took in both Tia and Kiki. "Am I understood?"

Tia nodded. Kiki did the same.

Nishell turned to Tia. "I got something else to say. You have so many good ideas. You a force. I want to be your friend. But when you do this kind of thing, it makes me not want to be your friend." She leaned in close. "Lemme tell you something, girlfriend. At our school, a girl needs her friends."

Tia nodded at Nishell. "I know that." Then she faced Kiki. "There's something I have to say to you, Kiki. All this really started when I told you I didn't want to share the scholarship with you. I still don't. You take that personally, but you shouldn't. I've seen you on the basketball court. You're fierce. You don't play to tie. You play to win. I play to win too. Play to win with me here, and let the best person win."

Kiki frowned. "It's not the same."

"It *is* the same. If you play fair, I'll play fair. In everything."

Ms. Okoro rubbed her chin. "I'm going to do a better job of making sure everyone plays fair. Now, who's with me on the YC team?"

She put her hand in the middle of the table. Nishell put hers on top of it. Sean did too.

Tia looked at Kiki. "What do you think?"

Kiki stared at the hands for a long time. Then finally, she said, "I'm in."

"Me too," Tia declared.

"I'll make sure everyone else is in too," Ms. O assured them. "I'll give a talk at the next meeting about how YC members must treat each other with respect. *All* YC members. The hip-hop artists call it, ' 'Nuff respect.' "

Slowly, Tia moved her closed fist across the table toward Kiki. Kiki met it halfway with her own. They fist-bumped. Tia grinned. So did Kiki.

"You're tough," Tia admitted. " 'Nuff respect."

"No tougher than you, you Bionic Latina diva. 'Nuff respect," Kiki fired back with a smile.

They laughed and bumped fists one more time. Then all of them locked hands. Nishell. Sean. Kiki. Ms. O. And Tia's atop them all.

YC was together again. Tia realized it was a much better place to be. It truly felt like home.